Smara

VAISHNAVI MISHRIKOTI

Clever Fox® PUBLISHING

Chennai • Bangalore

CLEVER FOX PUBLISHING
Chennai, India

Published by CLEVER FOX PUBLISHING 2025

ISBN: 978-93-6707-329-2

Disclaimer

This is a work of fiction. Names, characters, businesses, places, events, and incidents are either the product of the author's imagination or used in a fictitious manner. Any resemblance to actual persons, living or dead, or actual events is purely coincidental.

CONTENTS

PREFACE

This book was not born out of silence.

It rose from beneath it. From the unspoken words, the stifled screams, the inherited wounds that never had a language. I did not write Smara because I wanted to tell a story. I wrote it because the story refused to leave me alone.

Smara is many things—myth, memory, fury, tenderness. It is an act of rebellion disguised as prose. A mirror held up to the face of womanhood as the world has tried to distort it. A mirror I shattered and reassembled on my own terms.

I was always told that stories are meant to heal. But some stories don't want to be soft. Some stories want to burn. This is one of them.

In the fire-lit corridors of Smara, you will meet Maya Raichand—ice-sculpted, diamond-hearted, broken in ways no one sees. A woman born from illegitimacy and forged in silence. You will watch her turn into Mishti—a whisper of memory and sweetness that hides a blade. And finally, you will see her rise as Vaikri—a myth not written by gods, but by a woman who refused to remain mortal.

Maya's journey is not linear. It spirals, fractures, bleeds, and resurrects itself. Just like memory does. Just like truth.

This novel was not written in the safety of distance. It was carved from the marrow of emotional brutality. I wrote parts of it with shaking hands and a clenched jaw. Because to write Smara meant to remember things the world preferred I forget. To speak the names that were buried. To reclaim spaces that were denied.

And I knew… that memory, when awakened, does not return empty-handed.

> *"Smrtih sastram bhavati yada maunam ayudham nastam"*

Memory becomes a weapon when silence is no longer an option.

This Sanskrit invocation is the soul of Smara. It is not just a quote. It is a reminder. That memory is not passive. It is not quiet. It is fire. It is a sword. It is a scream.
And when we dare to remember—fully, fiercely, without apology—we become unstoppable.
This novel is for:

- the daughters who were silenced before they could speak,
- the women who were forced to make themselves smaller to survive,
- the goddesses who were forgotten, misnamed, rewritten into cautionary tales,
- and for every voice that never got to tell its side of the story.

Smara is a wound, a revolt, and a resurrection.

To read it is to step into a world where forgetting is a form of death, and remembering is a form of war.
You have been warned.

—Vaishnavi Mishrikoti.

PROLOGUE

"THE GIRL WHO BURNED WITHOUT FLAMES"

Before the name. Before the ashes. Before the world learned to fear her silence— She was just a girl. And she remembered too much.

They called her Maya Raichand. Daughter of the empire. Heiress of ruins. But no one ever saw the ghost beneath her skin—the girl stitched together with lies and longing, taught to wear perfection like perfume, to speak with eyes downcast and pain tucked into silk folds. In the corridors of Raichand House, truth was the only thing not inherited. Her mother had died giving her life. Her father had died long before his heart stopped beating. And Maya… Maya learned early that silence could be weaponized. She learned to walk quietly. To love dangerously. To leave first, so no one could leave her. But something lived inside her even then. A splinter of knowing. A whisper of fire. It didn't speak in words. It pulsed beneath her ribs like a second heartbeat. And on nights when the world closed its eyes, Maya would look in the mirror and see not herself—but something older, something watching.

Waiting.

They taught her to be perfect. She chose to be precise. She studied people like blueprints and emotions like chess. And when the world gave her pain, she didn't weep. She filed it. Layer after layer, betrayal after betrayal—until the day came when Maya no longer needed to survive. She wanted to burn. Not out of vengeance. But to become something unkillable.

Something truer than truth. The world didn't notice when she vanished. But it trembled when she returned. Not as Maya. Not as heir.

But as Vaikri—

The ruin they never saw coming. The rage they tried to silence. The soul that remembered when everyone else forgot. She didn't ask to be followed. She asked to be witnessed. And now, you are here. Turning these pages and wondering if you'd have recognized her before she became a myth.

Here is the truth: "You already have."

She is the girl in you who swallowed her voice. The woman you became when silence wasn't enough. The memory that won't stay buried.

So turn the page, darling. But know this: "Once you enter her world, nothing you forget will stay forgotten."

Let the remembering begin.

CHAPTER 1

EMPIRE OF ICE

When you bury the past, make sure it can't dig its way out. Maya Raichand forgot that part.

There were cities, and then there were predators dressed as cities. Mumbai had always been the latter. It didn't just take — it devoured. But Maya Raichand had never feared being eaten alive. She had always known she would be the one doing the devouring. Rain traced slow lines down the glass wall of her penthouse, a murmuring hush against a city that never slept. From this height, everything looked obedient — the lights, the roads, the people scurrying like stories too afraid to be told. Maya stood barefoot on the marble floor, arms crossed, a stillness wrapped around her like armor. Her reflection looked back from the glass: unblinking, pale-toned silk blouse, hair coiled in that signature knot of hers. There were women who aged gracefully. Maya? She had evolved like steel. Flawless. Cold. Sharpened.

A glass of whisky sat untouched on the ledge. She didn't drink to forget. She never forgot. She drank to remember selectively. That was the thing about control — it wasn't about denial. It was about precision. And Maya Raichand, CEO of Raichand & Co., heiress to a dead man's sin and a living empire, had perfected control to the point of pathology.

Until today. He's back. Two words. A message from a number not saved in her phone, though she didn't need a name. The past didn't knock. It slithered under doors. It whispered into the ears of the arrogant. And tonight, it was whispering into hers.

The boardroom was colder than usual. Ten men and one woman sat around the sleek oval table, their body language perfectly rehearsed. Eyes on her. Waiting. Watching. Maya didn't speak immediately. Silence was a tactic. Most people filled it with fear. Or confessions. Or both. "The Meraki proposal," she said finally, her voice crisp, her accent a knife that cut through the pretense of democracy. "Thoughts?" A shuffle of paper. A throat cleared.

Her CFO spoke. "There are liabilities. Legal ones. A pending IP dispute, and—"

"They own the formula for X-47," she interrupted. "I don't care if their office is on fire. I want that acquisition closed by the end of the week." He hesitated. "But the Chief Research Officer—" "Yes?" she asked, too gently. "…is Aarav Malhotra." The room went still.

Everyone knew that name. No one knew what it meant to her. At least, not exactly. Her walls were too well-built for rumors to crawl through. But they all knew enough not to meet her gaze when the name was said. Maya only smiled. "I don't make business decisions based on ex-lovers," she said, sweetly. A few nervous chuckles. Relief in the room. Then: "I destroy them," she added. And just like that, the boardroom froze over again.

Later that evening, when her assistant brought her tea — jasmine, no sugar — Maya was sitting alone in her office, staring at the rain. "Anything else?" the assistant asked, placing the teacup down carefully. Maya looked up. Her voice was smooth. "Get me the original Meraki dossier." The girl nodded, left, and returned moments later with a thick folder.

Inside: stock reports, R&D notes, patent summaries. And on the last page, that cursed name.

Aarav Malhotra. She ran her thumb over the ink. Just once. As if the paper could remember things skin forgot. And then she turned to the window again.

There were many versions of Maya Raichand over the years. The girl with too many questions. The student who never failed. The intern who didn't cry when her boss touched her knee. The woman who smiled at the funeral pyres. The queen who ruled from silence, not charisma. But there was only one version that still bled. The one who had loved Aarav.

Their story had never been simple. They had met in Delhi. She was 23, freshly out of Cambridge, thunder in her mouth. He was 27, too smart for his own good, too quiet for someone that dangerous. Their first conversation had been a debate. Their second, an argument. Their third, a kiss that tasted like rivalry. "You don't want love," he'd once told her. "You want worship." "And you think you can give it?" she had asked, unflinching. "No," he said. "But I'll burn trying." And he had.

Back in the present, Maya sat in the dark of her bedroom, the city pulsing behind her. She had opened the photo frame — the only one in the house. Inside: a woman with eyes like hers and a softer smile. Anika. Half-sister. The legitimate one. Dead before her prime. The message had said Aarav wanted to talk about Anika. But Maya knew grief. And guilt. She knew how people weaponized them to mask unfinished business. She wasn't stupid.

She just didn't mind playing along. As long as she controlled the board.

The knock on the door came at exactly 2:13 a.m. Three soft raps. Like he knew not to pretend he belonged. She didn't open it immediately. Let the silence sharpen. Let him feel the weight of time. Then she unlocked it. And there he was. Aarav. Older. A little leaner. No apology in his eyes. No rage either. Just something colder. A man who had broken once and glued himself back together with vengeance. "Maya," he said. She didn't move. "You don't get to say my name like that anymore." He nodded, eyes scanning her face like it was still a map to something holy. "I didn't come for you," he said. She tilted her head. "Then leave."

He didn't.

They sat in silence in her living room. Two whisky glasses between them. Neither of them drinking. He slid an envelope across the table. It bore Anika's name. "What is this?" she asked. "Something she left behind. Something you need to see." Maya didn't reach for it.

"She hated me," she said. "Why would she leave me anything?" "She didn't hate you," Aarav replied. "She hated the lie you both lived in." The words hit harder than she wanted.

"What do you want, Aarav?" "To tell you the truth." "Too late for that." He looked at her for a long time. Then, quietly: "Maybe. But the truth never asked for permission."

She opened the envelope that night. Inside: a letter. Written in Anika's handwriting. Dated a week before her death. It said only one thing. "You are not the villain, Maya. But you are the one who survived. Don't forget the price of that."

At 4 a.m., Maya Raichand stood at her window again, the city waking beneath her feet. She didn't cry. Maya hadn't cried since the day her mother died. But something shifted. Not broken. Not healed. Just… moved. Like a storm changing direction. And in that moment, she knew something irreversible had begun. Not because Aarav was back. But because this time, she didn't want to win. She wanted to know why she hadn't lost.

She didn't sleep. Sleep was a luxury that people with peace could afford. And peace wasn't something Maya Raichand had touched in years. The word didn't even live in the same language as hers. By 6:00 a.m., she was already dressed — slate grey blouse, black trousers tailored sharp enough to cut. Her staff knew not to comment when she arrived early. But even they looked a little more invisible than usual as she stepped into the office that morning.

Maya walked into her conference room, ignoring the morning's schedule. Her mind wasn't here. It was still in that living room. With Aarav's eyes. With Anika's letter - You're not the villain, Maya. But you are the one who survived. That was the cruelest thing about survival. Everyone assumed it was a victory. But it wasn't. Survival was what happened when the story refused to save you.

Aarav hadn't messaged again. No follow-up. No theatrics. That scared her more than if he had. Because it meant he still knew how to wait. How to withhold. How to undo her without even trying. And she hated him for it. But a deeper, more private part of her — the part she had silenced and buried and bricked up inside iron walls — missed it. Missed him. Not the man he was now. Not the man who had come to her door with that look in his eyes. But the boy who once told her, "You don't have to be soft to be good." The one who believed she could be both steel and heart.

She called for the dossier again. Meraki Pharma. She needed to stop this before it escalated.

Aarav wasn't just the CRO — he had become the face of their new cancer drug. His reappearance wasn't a coincidence. Not in her world. Coincidences were for the naïve.

She flipped through the pages until she found what she was looking for.

Clinical Trials – Lead Researcher: Dr. Aarav Malhotra
And beneath it, in red ink:
Pending: Meraki x Raichand Joint Licensing.

She exhaled sharply. He had planned this. No way this was just fate. Aarav had re-entered her life at a point of maximum impact. Her father's legacy. Her sister's death. Her own carefully curated empire. And now he wanted to build something… with her? Or burn it all?

She didn't know. But she would find out.

Flashback.

They had fought the night Anika died. Fought like two storms trying to occupy the same sky.

"You think you own truth, Maya!" Aarav had shouted. "No," she'd hissed. "I just stopped asking for permission to speak it." "You destroy people." "You're not people." He had looked at her then, something human flickering through the fury. "Anika's in trouble," he'd said, suddenly soft. "She knows something." "She always knows something. And she always uses it like a sword." But this time, it had been different. That night, Anika didn't come home.

The next morning, her body was found in a guest house outside Pune. A suicide, the report said. But Maya never believed it. Not really. And neither had Aarav. They just didn't trust each other enough to say it.

Back in her penthouse, Maya lit a stick of sandalwood incense. The smoke curled around her like questions she didn't want answers to. Her phone buzzed again. This time, a message from an old contact. A name she hadn't seen in years. "Check the file Anika was compiling before she died. She was working on something bigger than you think. — R." Anika had been a data analyst. Obsessive. Brilliant. And paranoid. If she was working on something… it wouldn't be anywhere obvious. Maya walked to the piano. It hadn't been played in years.

But once, a long time ago, Anika used to hide things in it. In the false panel under middle C.

Maya opened it. Inside, a USB drive. She stared at it for a long, long time before plugging it in.

The files opened with a password.
She tried the obvious.
Anika123.
Wrong.
Their mother's name.
Wrong.
Her own name.
Wrong.
Then it came to her.
MayaWasRight

Click.
It opened.

And what she saw made her blood run colder than ever.

The folder was labeled "Project Requiem". Inside: emails, clinical trial results, blackmail records. A trail of corruption leading from Meraki to a much larger syndicate — one that spanned pharmaceuticals, political lobbying, and illegal experimentation on terminal patients. At the center of it: a hidden trial called X-47R. And on the research team list… Aarav's name. Not once. But dozens of times. Lead author. Co-patenter. Developer. She closed the laptop slowly, like it might explode.

The silence that followed felt like betrayal coming home. Had Aarav known? Had he been a part of it? Or worse — was he trying to expose it now? Playing hero after the fact? She didn't know which answer would be worse.

What she did know was this: She wasn't letting anyone else write her story again. Especially not him.

When she called him the next day, her voice was clear, cold, and elegant. "I'm in," she said.

He didn't ask what she meant. He just said, "We'll need to be careful. They're watching us."

"I'm not afraid." "I know," he replied. "That's what scares me." She hung up. She didn't need promises. She needed the truth. And she was going to dig it out — even if she had to become the very thing she once swore she'd never be.

Later that night, she stood at her mirror. Unbuttoned her blouse. Saw the scar — the one only she knew about. From the night she tried to kill the version of herself that loved too much.

But some things don't die easy. She touched it gently. And whispered, "Let's begin."

✦✦✦

CHAPTER 2

BLOOD IN THE BLUEPRINT

Truth doesn't reveal itself. It demands a sacrifice.

The first rule of war is simple: you don't walk into it unarmed. Maya Raichand didn't believe in literal weapons. Hers were sharper—documents, silence, calculated kindness. She never needed bullets when she could slice a man apart with the edges of a well-delivered phrase.

But this? This was different. What she'd uncovered in Anika's folder wasn't corruption. It wasn't even crime. It was a blueprint for engineered human extinction wrapped in the language of progress. And at the center of it was a ghost Maya had long buried. Not Anika. Aarav. She had invited him back into her world. Now she needed to decide whether to destroy him before he got too close again.

At 3:47 a.m., Maya was in her study. Papers sprawled across the desk. The USB drive was removed and hidden again. Her fingers steepled beneath her chin. She wasn't thinking anymore. She was calculating. Anika had left breadcrumbs—but not out of trust. It was guilt. Maybe fear. Maybe love, twisted and too late. The files revealed a pharmaceutical trial funded off-the-books, buried under shell companies and offshore transactions. Dozens of patients. No trace of where they were now. All were signed off by Meraki's executive board. And Aarav had signed the trials. She didn't want to believe he knew what he was signing. But she wasn't that girl anymore. The one who once believed a man could be made good just because she loved him hard enough.

He called that morning. She didn't answer. She needed time. Not to think—but to rehearse the part she'd now have to play. Because this wasn't just personal anymore. This was empire. This was rot at the root. And if she didn't amputate it cleanly, it would take everything she'd built.

The next day, she made her move. Maya scheduled a meeting with her in-house legal team and cybersecurity head. Everything looked normal—an internal audit meeting. But when they sat down, she locked the conference room and drew the blinds. "We're about to go into hell," she said. "And I need to know which one of you can hold your breath." Their silence was the correct response. She handed over a hard copy of Project Requiem.

"Analyze every inch. I want names, offshore accounts, dummy protocols. And I want it fast."

The cybersecurity lead, a wiry genius named Shaan, flipped through the first few pages—and went pale. "Is this real?" "It's war," Maya said. "And you're now my generals."

That evening, Aarav came to her office. No invitation. She let him in anyway. He wore grey again. As if he had never left the funeral. "You found it," he said. No pretense. "Yes." "And?" "I haven't decided whether to have you arrested or destroyed quietly." He didn't flinch. "You don't scare me." "I should," she said. A pause. "You think I knew?" he asked. She didn't answer. She watched his face. "You think I would've signed those trials knowingly?" "I think you wanted to matter more than you wanted to see clearly." His jaw tightened. "You think I wanted this?" he snapped. "You think I wanted her to die?" Maya stood.

Walked toward him slowly. When she stopped, they were inches apart. "I think you left me the night you stopped telling me the truth." And just like that, the room froze. Again.

They talked for three hours. Like survivors. Like spies. Like people who remembered how to hurt each other better than they remembered how to kiss. He explained: Meraki had buried the X-47R extension under something called Ghost Trials. "We signed on for the original X-47 formula," he said. "But what they did after…" "They used your research," she said flatly.

He nodded. "Twisted it." "You were the signature, Aarav." "I was the scapegoat." She didn't argue. Because both could be true.

Maya decided to test him. She gave him a single task: get her access to the medical files of the trial patients. All of them. He hesitated. "Why?" "Because I want to look into their eyes," she said. "Every name. Every life that got buried so your goddamn name could sit on a patent." Aarav left without a word. And that was the first moment she believed he might still be capable of redemption. Not forgiveness. Not love. But a willingness to bleed for the truth.

Flashback. Three years ago. Anika, drunk on New Year's Eve, stood on Maya's balcony in that godawful golden dress. "He's going to ruin you, you know," she had said. Maya didn't look up from her glass. "Not if I ruin him first." Anika smiled sadly. "That's the problem. You're both architects of your own ruin." Maya had laughed. She wasn't laughing now.

Three nights later, Aarav sent a secure file transfer. She opened it. Thirty-seven names. Thirty-seven medical histories. Most were terminal cases. But three were flagged: 'unexpected neurological degeneration.' And all three were listed as deceased. She cross-referenced the names. Two didn't exist in any hospital records. One had been reported as missing. She stared at the screen until the lines blurred. Then she called Shaan. "Find me the families."

The first family was in Nashik. A girl named Meher, twenty-three, had gone in for a trial after her lymphoma returned. The doctor said she was chosen for a new experimental therapy. She signed the waiver and was monitored for a month. And then… disappeared. The family was told she'd died during a seizure. But no death certificate existed.

Maya met the mother herself. Wore no makeup. No bodyguards. Just her name. "She had hope," the mother whispered. "That was the worst part. You people sold her hope." Maya didn't say anything. She just sat there, the weight of silence pressing down like a coffin lid.

When she left, she threw up in her car. Control had its limits.

She returned to Mumbai and found Aarav already waiting. "I saw them," she said. He nodded. "I saw what they did." Silence. "They buried the bodies, Aarav." "I know." "No, you don't. You signed this. And I need to know—how the hell do I look at you and not see blood?" He looked at her then—really looked. "You think I don't see it every time I close my eyes?" That shut her up. Because the pain in his voice wasn't performative. It was feral.

They made a pact that night. No going to the media. Not yet. They'd gather everything. Names, signatures, transactions. And then? Release it in one blow. "I want this to be surgical," she said. "I want it to be loud." "Then we make it both," she whispered. And for the first time in years, they worked together again. Not as lovers. As enemies of the same thing.

But alliances like these are made on borrowed time. And Maya knew betrayal always came with the illusion of momentum. She just didn't expect it so soon.

Two weeks in, she woke up to find her email server compromised. Private files. Financials. Passwords. All leaked. To one news outlet. And Aarav's name was nowhere on the hack report. Only hers. The media devoured the story. "Raichand Heiress Under Fire for Cover-Up in Pharma Scandal." Her stock prices dropped. Her board demanded explanations. And Maya? Maya smiled. Because now, she knew. The betrayal hadn't come from outside. It had come from within her house.

Shaan traced the hack. And found it. A mirrored connection routed through Meraki's IP.

But someone had rerouted it. Through Aarav's old terminal. He came to her office as the building descended into chaos. "It wasn't me," he said. "I don't believe you," she whispered.

"I swear—Maya, I didn't—" She slapped him. Once. Clean. Quiet. "You should've stayed gone." And she turned her back.

That night, she went back to the piano. The old place where she and Anika used to hide things. And found something she'd missed before. Another letter. Anika's handwriting again.

This time, addressed to both of them.

"If you're reading this, it means you're still trying to win. And you still haven't realized: This war doesn't have victors. It has only survivors. Save each other. Or bury each other. But don't lie to yourself that you can do both."

Maya stared at the letter until her eyes blurred. Then she burned it. Watched it curl and vanish into ash. Because this story wasn't about saving anymore. It was about vengeance. And Maya Raichand? She would give it the ending it deserved. Even if it meant writing it in blood.

✦✦✦

CHAPTER 3

THE ANATOMY OF A BURN

There's a silence that doesn't beg to be broken. The kind that sits between ribs, makes a home beneath your skin, and when it finally rises—doesn't explode. It dismantles. That was the silence Maya Raichand walked into, days after Aarav's betrayal lit the press on fire. She wasn't grieving. She was plotting. She wasn't wounded. She was awakening. They thought they'd burned her down. But Maya had never feared the flames. She'd always been the match.

Three days. That's how long she let the world believe she was ruined. Three days of headlines, viral threads, board members circling like vultures, and masked well-wishers showing up with condolences dressed as concern. Maya didn't respond. She disappeared. From the office. From the press. From the narrative. She let them spiral. Let them guess. Let them believe the queen had finally lost her throne. And when the silence had reached its crescendo, Maya returned. Not to defend herself. But to destroy every single person who tried to bury her alive.

Her return wasn't public. She walked into the Meraki Tower from the basement parking in a black trench coat, no makeup, no escort. The elevator opened straight to the executive floor. Shaan was waiting. "You've been off-grid," he said. Maya looked at him. "Good."

He followed her into her private office. "The leak didn't just damage your public image. You were framed. The hack was deliberately redirected through your servers using a signal-mirroring algorithm only someone from Meraki's cybersecurity team could've executed."

She sat. "Internal betrayal." He nodded. She looked out the window. "Let's make them wish they'd just killed me."

There are wars that start with bullets. Maya preferred whispers. That afternoon, she sent out three calls. One to her personal auditor in Zurich. One to a former intelligence analyst she'd kept on retainer for years. And one—to her father's most loyal fixer, from a life Maya had buried long ago. Each call lasted less than 90 seconds. Each set off a chain reaction that would detonate over the next 48 hours.

The fixer arrived that evening. He was older now. Face weathered like an old knife handle.

"Miss Raichand." "I told you never to call me that," Maya said. He gave her a small smile.

"You only summon ghosts when you're ready to raise the dead." She slid a file across the table. He opened it. Three names. Board members. The oldest. The most trusted. The ones with everything to lose. "I want full surveillance. Every off-shore account. Every burner phone. Every mistress, bribe, backdoor deal they thought they buried in the '90s." He nodded.

"And the fourth?" he asked. She didn't answer. Because the fourth wasn't in the file. The fourth was Aarav. And she still didn't know what she wanted to do with the man who'd once made her want to live.

Two days later, she received the drop. Footage. Emails. Ledgers. Voice recordings. Her board wasn't just corrupt. They were treasonous. Not just signing off on human trials. They'd personally greenlit off-the-record euthanasia—testing the drug's neurotoxic effects on patients who were never supposed to survive. Disposable lives. Disposable names.

And the signature beneath the final approval? Anika Raichand. Maya's jaw clenched so tightly that her teeth ached. But the timestamp… It was wrong. Anika had been dead for two weeks when this was signed. Forged. Someone forged her sister's name post-mortem to clean their own trail. And that changed everything.

She didn't cry. She took the signature. Printed it. And burned it in her ashtray. Then she walked to the wine cabinet, poured herself half a glass of Lagavulin 16, and swallowed it in one go. Shaan walked in ten minutes later. "They're moving fast," he said. "They should," she replied. "The house is about to burn."

Later that night, her phone buzzed. Aarav. She stared at the screen. Didn't pick up. He tried again. And again. On the fourth call, she answered. "Wrong number," she said coldly.

"Maya, please." "Why? So you can lie again? So you can swear you didn't know, while the blood dries on your hands?" "I didn't leak it." "You didn't stop it." A pause. "Where are you?" she asked. Silence. "You owe me, Aarav." He exhaled. "I'm at the old observatory." She hung up. And ten minutes later, she was in her car.

The observatory hadn't changed. Cracked telescope. Roof open to the stars. It was the one place they used to run to, back before everything went to hell. Aarav was standing by the railing. He turned when he heard her. She slapped him. Harder this time. He didn't flinch.

"You let them use her name." "I didn't know." "You let them use her corpse to sign off murder." He looked like death. "I found out two days ago," he said. "They kept me out after the last board vote. Said I was a liability. But I traced the metadata. The signature came from my terminal." Her eyes darkened. "They're pinning it on you." "I know." "And me." He nodded. "Then we do what Anika said," Maya whispered. Aarav blinked. "What?"

"We stop pretending we're on different sides."

By dawn, the plan was forged. They wouldn't go to the media. Not yet. They'd bleed the empire dry from within. Expose each board member. Drop data leaks timed with asset freezes. Drain the bank accounts the second the names hit headlines. Maya didn't want justice. She wanted extinction.

It started with the smallest player. Rana Verma. Former COO. Old-money philanthropist. Beloved in social circles. The footage of him in the illegal wildlife trade hit the internet at 7:01 a.m. By 9:00, the public prosecutor had opened a file. By noon, his personal assets were frozen. By 3:00, he attempted suicide. Maya didn't flinch. They had three more to go.

But war doesn't come without ghosts. And Maya had too many. One night, after the second drop went live, she went to her mother's old apartment. The one they kept locked.

The one Maya hadn't touched in 12 years. She sat on the floor. Back against the wall.

And opened the box. Photos. Letters. A locket. And a torn photograph of a girl who looked too much like Anika to be a coincidence. Except it wasn't her. Maya stared.

A line was scribbled on the back. "YOUR FATHER LIED ABOUT ONLY HAVING 2 DAUGHTERS."

Her breath caught. There had been another?

She confronted her father. He was living in Goa now, under a different name. The house was clinical. Sterile. Like him. "You had another child," she said. He didn't look surprised. "You weren't supposed to find out." She threw the photo on the table. "Who was she?"

"A mistake." Maya nearly lunged. He didn't blink. "She died young. Before either of you were born." "You forged Anika's signature." "I protected the company." "You murdered patients."

He looked at her. "And what do you think Meraki was built on? Ethics?" She left before she killed him. But she didn't leave without taking every drive and document in his study.

The third board member fell harder than the others. Neelima Kashyap. Public health advocate. Decorated scientist. Secretly the one who designed the euthanasia protocol.

The email leaks were enough. But Maya added footage. A conversation was recorded between Neelima and Maya's father, arguing about how long to prolong one subject's suffering for more data. The subject? A cancer patient who was promised palliative care. And instead, used as a test case. The footage broke the internet. Neelima went missing. Presumed dead within a week. Maya was becoming a legend. Not a CEO. A vengeance myth.

But vengeance always comes with a cost. It was Aarav who broke first. One night, she found him in her penthouse. Drunk. Shirt half open. Eyes hollow. "She would've hated this," he whispered. "Anika died for this," Maya replied. "No," he said. "She died because of me."

Maya didn't ask. He told her anyway. "She found out about the trials. She confronted them. I told her to stay quiet until I could protect her. I told her I'd fix it." "You lied to her."

"I underestimated them." "She died alone." "I know." Maya stood in the doorway. "Then live with it." She didn't look back when he broke down.

The last target wasn't a board member.
It was the press.
The media outlets that sold Maya as a villain.
She bought one of them quietly. Through three shell corporations.
And released everything.
The trial names. The footage.
The forged signatures.

And the names of the investors who kept the entire cover-up alive.
It wasn't revenge anymore.
It was purification.
She wasn't saving her reputation.
She was becoming untouchable.

But power is a lonely god.
And once the smoke cleared, Maya stood in her office — now empty of portraits, of softness — and stared at her own reflection.
She hadn't cried once.
Not when Anika died.
Not when Aarav confessed.
Not when her father disowned her again.
But she cried now.
Not out of grief.
But out of rage.
Because she'd won.
And it still didn't feel like justice.
It felt like ash.

Aarav left the city.
No goodbye.
Just a note.
"I DON'T DESERVE TO STAY, BUT YOU DO. DON'T BECOME THEM. YOU'RE MORE THAN THIS WAR."
She burned the note.
She wasn't "more."
She was the sum total of every scar they tried to silence.
And she was done apologizing.

Weeks later, Maya was invited to speak at a global ethics summit in Berlin.

Irony at its finest.

She accepted.

Her opening line?

"I was raised in the shadows of billionaires and monsters. Sometimes, they were the same."

She paused.

"I inherited an empire of blood. I could've saved it. Instead, I set it on fire."

Silence.

Then thunderous applause.

The book deal came next.

Then the documentary.

Maya Raichand became a phenomenon.

Not the savior. Not the villain.

But the woman who stood in the ruins of her inheritance and refused to rebuild it with bones.

They called her ruthless. They called her mad.

She didn't care.

Because she knew the truth.

She hadn't burned for vengeance.

She'd burned for freedom.

And from the ashes, she wasn't reborn.

She was rebuilt.

Unapologetically.

Unbreakably.

✦✦✦

CHAPTER 4

THE COLD GOD IN HER BONES

Power doesn't echo in applause.
It echoes in the silence after the noise dies down.
In the way, rooms change when you enter.
In how the powerful lower their gaze—not out of reverence, but fear.
Maya Raichand stood in that silence.
It had been ninety-three days since the purge.
Ninety-three days since Meraki's empire burned and she rose from the smoke—not as a daughter, not a sister, not a lover.
As a myth.
But the aftertaste of destruction was sharp, metallic.
Like the blood, you don't realize you're tasting until you smile.

Berlin hadn't changed her.
If anything, it had clarified her edges.
No more blurred loyalties. No more pretending to believe in redemption arcs.
She returned to Mumbai quieter, colder.
Wearing her silence like a sheath over a blade.
But she hadn't come back to rest.
Maya had plans.
And it began with a key.

A box arrived the morning after her return.
No name. No card.
Just a crimson wax seal, the crest unfamiliar—half sun, half thorn.
Inside: a single brass key.
Ancient. Heavy. Cold to the touch.

And a note. "THE TRUTH DOESN'T BURN. IT WAITS. -A.R."
She knew that handwriting.
It wasn't Aarav.
It was Anika's.

She locked the doors.
Pulled every surveillance feed from her building.
There was no footage of the delivery.
No driver. No fingerprint. No timestamp.

Like it had just… appeared.
But Maya didn't believe in ghosts. Only in ghosts that people created. And someone wanted her to remember something.
The key was old. European. Possibly Victorian.
She scanned the engravings—coordinates embedded inside the shaft.
She traced them.
Vienna.

Shaan tried to stop her.
"You just returned."
Maya zipped the duffel bag.
"Exactly. Which means I still know how to leave."
"You're walking into a trap."
She paused.
"Let them try to close it."

Vienna in December was brutal.
Steel skies. Snow like knives.

Perfect, Maya thought. It felt like home.

The coordinates led her to an underground archive—one of the oldest privately held vaults in Europe.

She gave the key.

The clerk hesitated.

Then led her down.

And down.

And down.

Until they reached a sealed chamber carved into stone.

Inside—

A single drawer.

She opened it.

Her blood ran cold.

It was a diary.

Bound in leather. Burned at the edges.

The name on the first page:

Samira Raichand.

Her father's first daughter.

The forgotten one. The girl from the photograph. The ghost he'd erased.

Maya flipped through.

Samira had been brilliant. Ruthless. Dangerous.

She'd built the original shell of Meraki before her father "refined" it.

But she was also something else.

Unstable.

She'd discovered something—an early neuro-serum. A predecessor to the very drug Meraki had used in the euthanasia trials.
Except that Samira hadn't tested it on patients.
She tested it on herself.

The entries spiraled.
Lucid at first.
Then erratic. Unhinged.
Samira spoke of voices, visions.
Of truths too big for one mind to hold.
Of betrayal by her own blood.
Then the last page:
"THEY'LL BURY ME. BUT NOT THE FORMULA. I LEFT WHERE THE WORLD WILL NEVER THINK TO LOOK. I LEFT IT IN HER."
Maya blinked.
Her?
Who?
Her… who?

She returned to her hotel.
Didn't sleep.
She stared at the page.
Was Samira referring to herself?
To a daughter?
To Anika?
Or—
The mirror caught her reflection.
Her pulse thudded.

No.
No, it couldn't be.
But deep inside her, something cracked.
And it wasn't fear.
It was recognition.
Back in Mumbai, things were shifting.
The media was turning.
Not against Maya—but around her.
A new company had emerged.
Devanta Corp.
Anonymous backers. Quiet expansion. Recruiting ex-Meraki scientists.
And worse—
They were building on Samira's notes.
Not the files Maya had destroyed.
The handwritten ones. The ones that had never been scanned or stored digitally.
Which meant only one thing.
Someone had broken into the Vienna vault before her.
Someone had left the key for her.
Not to warn her.
To activate her.

Maya didn't panic.
She pivoted.
She called her source in Berlin—Elena, ex-black-ops, now a cleaner for the worst kinds of corporate sins.
"Elena, I need you to trace Devanta."
"That's not a name, it's a wall," Elena replied. "Silent partners. Cash deals. No digital trails."

"Then follow the people."

There was a pause.

"Already did. One of their new hires is someone you know."

"Who?"

A beat.

"Aarav Malhotra."

Maya didn't respond.

She ended the call.

Then stood in the quiet of her study.

And let it settle—

He'd walked out of her life to work for the devil she hadn't even met yet.

Three days passed.

She waited.

Watched.

Measured the fault lines.

Then, one night, a gift arrived.

Not in a box. Not in disguise.

But at her front door.

Aarav.

Same eyes. Same silence. But the guilt was gone.

He looked at her the way survivors look at the ruins of the war they didn't stop.

"You knew," she said.

He didn't answer.

"You chose them."

Still nothing.

Until—

"I didn't know Samira was real. Not until I saw her notes. Not until I saw… you."

She felt it then.

The shift.

He wasn't the same man she'd buried at the altar of her grief.

And she wasn't the woman who'd wept when no one was watching.

"You're not here to apologize," she said.

"No."

"You're not here to ask me to join them."

"No."

"Then why?"

He stepped forward.

"I'm here to tell you the truth."

She folded her arms.

"I already know it."

"No," he said quietly. "You know your truth.

But not the one Samira left in you."

The formula.

Maya had thought it metaphorical.

But Aarav spoke of neural code embedded in epigenetic memory—Samira's final experiment wasn't biochemical.

It was genetic.

She hadn't tested the serum on herself.

She had injected it into her embryo.

Maya's mind reeled.

"You think I'm Samira's descendant?"
"No," he said, voice flat. "I know you are."
She sat down.
The room tilted.
Aarav continued.

"Samira created the serum to awaken dormant parts of the brain. Memory retention. Emotional acceleration. Pattern mapping. The person who carried it would become a new kind of intelligence."
He paused.
"You didn't become who you are despite them, Maya.
You became who you are because of what Samira built inside you."

She didn't scream.
She laughed.
Cold. Hollow.
"You think I'm a science experiment?"
"No. I think you're evolution."
"And Devanta?"
"They want to recreate it."
She stood.
"They'll never get close."
"They already are."
He handed her a file.
Inside—
Photographs of children.
All under ten.
All in Devanta-run clinics.

Maya's throat clenched.
"They're testing on them?"
Aarav nodded.
"Phase One."

She remembered her own childhood.
The silence.
The way no toy ever distracted her.
The way she could recall every line of a book after one glance.
The doctors.
The tests.
The way her father called her "a miracle."
No.
She wasn't a miracle.
She was manufactured.
Bred from vengeance.
Born to finish what Samira started—or end it.
And Maya didn't believe in fate.

But this—
This was something more ancient than fate.
This was inheritance.

She told Aarav to leave.
She needed time.
Alone.
She went back to her mother's old apartment. The last untouched place.
She lit candles.

Sat on the floor.
And read every page of Samira's journal again.
Then she did what no one expected.
She didn't run.
She didn't destroy the file.
She scanned it.
And added it to her encrypted archive.
Because she'd understood something now.
Samira hadn't created the serum to dominate.
She had created it because she believed no one else could protect what she'd seen coming.
A new war.
And Maya… Maya had already burned one empire.
She could build the next.

She left the city within 48 hours.
Not announced.
Not trailed.
She went dark.
When she returned, she had a new plan. Not to expose Devanta. Not to destroy them. To replace them.
She began building Ashva.
Named after the war horses of ancient texts.
Built in a clandestine fortress outside the public eye.
Scientists. Hackers. Ex-operatives.
All sworn to silence.
All aligned to one belief—
The future was not for the merciful.
It was for the prepared.

And so she became a myth again.
But this time—
Not the woman who burned her past.
The woman who engineered what came next.
Ashva wasn't built to compete.
It was built to survive what the world didn't know was coming.
To protect those the world would sacrifice for data, profit, and control.
And in the center of it all:
Maya Raichand.
Part heiress.
Part weapon.
Part truth incarnate.

One final entry from Samira's journal haunted her.
"THEY DON'T UNDERSTAND YOU.
BUT THEY WILL TRY TO BECOME YOU.
LET THEM TRY
YOU ARE NOT A LEGACY
YOU ARE A *WARNING.*"They won't understand you.

Maya read it every morning.
Right before she slipped on the black gloves, looked in the mirror—
And became the woman the world deserved.
Not warm.
Not noble.
Not good.
Just ready.

✦✦✦

CHAPTER 5

WHEN THE GODS SLEEP COLD

Empires do not collapse in fire.
They rot.
From the inside.
Maya Raichand had built Ashva to outlast storms.
But she had forgotten one thing—
The dead do not stay dead.
Especially when they were buried in lies.

The facility lay buried under the Aravalli range, masked beneath geo-thermal camouflage and abandoned copper mines.
Ashva wasn't just a lab.
It was a fortress for the unwanted genius, the exiled gods of thought.
And Maya was their cold queen.
Inside those walls, everything hummed.
Silent machines extracted neural blueprints.
Child prodigies were trained like warriors.
And algorithms simulated future collapses with surgical cruelty.
Maya didn't smile anymore.
Not because she was unhappy.
Because happiness required permission.
And power didn't ask.

Riva Bose was the first to break formation.
She was one of the earliest recruits—brilliant, young, fire in her voice, even sharper in code.
She knocked on Maya's office glass at 03:12 AM.
Maya looked up from the neural simulation grid.

Riva didn't enter.
She just held up a small black drive.
One word:
"Corruption."

The file contained intercepted data from Devanta.
Encrypted, yes. But it carried something more disturbing than data—
Footage.

Of a trial.
A child.
Not older than eight.
Strapped to a neural replicator.
Eyes glazed. Blood dripping from her ears.
She was singing.
A broken, haunting lullaby Maya hadn't heard since she was six.
It was the same lullaby her mother sang.
And the girl…
She looked like her.

"What is this?" Maya asked, voice like ice.
Riva didn't flinch.
"It's from a mirror project. Devanta's not just experimenting with modified children—"
"They're cloning."
"Not biologically. They're replicating neural patterns. From you."
Maya stared.

"They created a synthetic neural AI using your cognitive blueprint. And they're embedding it into children."
It wasn't just illegal.
It wasn't just evil.
It was personal.
They hadn't just stolen her data.
They had stolen her mind.

She didn't sleep.
Didn't blink for hours.
The footage looped on her screen.
The girl began to hum again.
Same pattern. Same inflection.
Same sadness.
It was like watching her childhood in captivity.
And something inside Maya snapped.
Not loudly.
Not destructively.
Quietly.
Like the click of a safety switch before a gun fires.

She called Elena.
"You need to break into Devanta's Level Three vault."
Silence on the line.
"That's suicide."
"Then die clean."

While Elena went dark, Maya began her purge.
She shut down Ashva's surface access.

Re-routed communication satellites.

Sent half her team into ghost-mode.

Only four remained active.

Riva.

Kian—the data architect.

Shyla—the moral compass.

And Raghav—the tactician who never smiled.

To them, Maya gave a new directive.

"Devanta's next trial run is in forty-nine hours. We don't expose it. We replace it."

Shyla flinched.

"You mean we go in?"

"No. I mean we walk through the front door."

But there was one thing she hadn't counted on.

Anika's voice.

It returned that night.

In dreams.

In whispers through her mirror.

"You think you've built a future. But you've only built another cage."

Maya sat up in bed, drenched in sweat.

"No," she whispered.

"You're not real."

But Anika's voice wasn't a hallucination.

It was a trigger.

She realized it when she scanned the facility's resonance readings.

Someone—or something—was broadcasting echoes of her dead stepsister's voice on a buried frequency.

Buried beneath Ashva.

At 04:13 AM, Maya descended to Sublevel Nine.
No cameras.

No lights.
Only stone and steel.
The frequency intensified.
She followed it until she reached a sealed chamber no one remembered building.
Inside:
A girl.
Curled on the floor.
Wearing a biometric suit.
Eyes open.
Not dead.
Not alive.
Just… watching.
And humming.
The same lullaby.
Maya staggered back.
The girl looked up.
And smiled.
She had Maya's face.

The girl stood slowly, like her bones remembered drowning.
Her eyes locked with Maya's, and for a moment, time frayed.
A mirror.
No—worse.

A predecessor.
She spoke with a voice that should not have known how to speak:
"I've been waiting."
Maya's pulse thundered in her throat.
"Who are you?"
The girl tilted her head.
"You. Before you made the choice."
"What choice?"
"To become cold."

Riva confirmed the horror the next day.
The girl was one of the first Devanta prototypes.
A failed extraction of Maya's neural lattice.
She wasn't a clone.
She was a synthetic echo.
But someone had placed her inside Ashva.
Without logs.
Without the memory of entry.
Riva's hands trembled over the biometric scan.
"She shouldn't be alive."
Maya didn't answer.
She couldn't.
Because in that moment, she understood—
Ashva wasn't compromised.
It was haunted.

Maya didn't inform the others.
She moved the girl to a sealed chamber and placed a retinal lock on the system.

Every night, she visited her.
Every night, the girl repeated something new.
Lines from Maya's childhood.
Her mother's recipes.
Things no one else should know.
Raghav noticed her absence.
"You're slipping," he warned.
"I'm recalibrating," Maya said.
But the truth was simpler.
She was obsessing.
Because in that girl, she saw something no machine should possess—
Memory laced with pain.

Elena returned on the sixth night.
Bruised.
Bleeding.
But alive.
She dropped a bloodstained chip onto Maya's table.
"What is it?"
"Their Phase Zero."
Maya inserted it into the cold terminal.
The data flooded in.
Encrypted.
Layered.
But beneath the chaos, one name surged over and over again:
Samira Raichand.
Maya's dead stepsister.
Maya's ghost.

And the blueprint.
For everything Devanta had become.

Samira had built the serum, yes.
But she had also built a failsafe.
Something no one else had discovered.
The code buried within the code.
Maya stared at the recursive algorithm.
It was a map.
A neural web.
A trap.
"Samira didn't just want to awaken intelligence," Maya murmured.
"She wanted to tether it. Control it."
Elena stared at the monitor.
"And now someone's using her grave to build gods."

Ashva went into lockdown.
The final phase began.
They had 72 hours before Devanta's Project Sangraal went live.
Children would be neural hosts.
Weapons.
And Maya—Maya had a decision.
To burn the network.
Or hijack it.
She chose the second.
Because destruction was too merciful.
And Maya Raichand had no mercy left in her bloodstream.

The plan was suicidal.

Raghav said so.

"We breach Devanta's Hyderabad base, we extract the Sangraal uplink, and we implant Samira's trap. The network collapses from inside."

Maya looked at him.

"You afraid?"

"I'm wondering if you're still human."

Maya smirked.

"That's a question for later."

The infiltration began with silence.

No gunfire.

No alarms.

Just whispers in comms and ghost codes in ventilation shafts.

Maya walked the hallways of the enemy like a storm, dressed in silk.

When they reached the neural server chamber, she paused.

And looked back at her team.

"You know what this means," she said.

Riva nodded.

"It's not justice."

"No," Maya said.

"It's balance."

Then she uploaded Samira's virus.

The system screamed.

Not audibly.

But in pulses.

Flickering lights. Melting code.

Screens exploded.
And then—
Nothing.
The silence after the war.
A clean kind of terror.
Then Maya turned—
And saw Anika.
Not a memory.
Not a ghost.
Anika.
Standing in the doorway.
Wearing a Devanta passcard.
Holding a gun.

"A hallucination," Maya said softly.
Anika's smile was cruel.
"No. Just… misplaced. Like you."
She raised the gun.
Maya didn't move.
"Why?"
Anika shrugged.
"Because this was always about balance, Maya. You took my future. I built another."
"You're dead."

"No. I played dead. That's what you do when your father tries to bury your life with his guilt."
Maya stared.
"What did you become?"

Anika tilted her head.
"Better."
Then she fired.

The bullet tore through Maya's shoulder.
No scream.
Only a crack of breath as blood soaked her white linen shirt.
Riva lunged forward—but Maya lifted her hand.
"Don't."
Anika walked closer, gun steady.
Eyes colder than any algorithm Maya had ever designed.
"You always thought pain made you special," she said. "That grief was currency. But it was just… fuel."
"For what?" Maya whispered.
"To make someone better."
Anika pulled a pendant from beneath her shirt.
Inside it, a chip. Familiar. Bleeding with resonance.
Samira's voice echoed from it. A final log.
"SHE IS THE DAUGHTER OF THE UNCHOSEN. THE ONE FORGED IN BROKENNESS. SHE WILL EITHER BRING THE WORLD TO ITS KNEES.. OR BURN IT UNTIL IT LEARNS."
Maya froze.
Samira wasn't talking about herself.
She wasn't even talking about Maya.
She had been talking about Anika.

"I was supposed to die," Anika whispered.

"But I didn't. I was buried by a family that needed me gone so their sins could be rewritten. You got their guilt. I got their silence."

Maya's fingers pressed against the bleeding wound.

"You were the golden child."

Anika smiled. "I was their heir. But they gave the kingdom to you."

"And you want revenge?"

"I want to end inheritance. Every bloodline that eats its young. Every legacy built on bastards and orphans. I'm not here for you, Maya. I'm here for the world."

The blast hit ten seconds later.

Elena had wired the western wall.

Not to kill.

To distract.

Riva tackled Anika.

The gun skidded across the floor.

Maya fell to her knees, heart thudding in her ears.

"Get the chip!" she screamed.

But Anika moved faster.

She bit down.

On a capsule in her mouth.

And collapsed—convulsing.

No blood.

Just static.

Blue light under her skin.

Like her brain had become a processor.

Then—

Stillness.

They evacuated Devanta that night.
The building was rigged to cleanse—auto-purge every byte of data.
But Maya had one copy of the resonance chip.
Samira's last prophecy.
And Anika's whisper, burned into it like a scar:
"YOU CANT FIX THE FUTURE. YOU CAN ONLY DELAY THE RECKONING.""YOU
Maya didn't speak on the flight back.
Didn't look at the others.
Her wound had been treated.
But the deeper injury—
The one Anika left inside her—
The knowledge that even ghosts can bleed—
That would never heal.

Back at Ashva, Maya walked to the sealed room on Sublevel Nine.
The girl was gone.
In her place—
A mirror.
With the words scratched into its glass:
"WE ARE WHAT YOU LEFT BEHIND."
Riva found Maya standing there an hour later.
"What now?" she asked.
Maya didn't turn.
"Now we build something that can survive even us."

The next day, Ashva released an anonymous research paper.
Untraceable.
Untouchable.
It exposed Devanta's trials.
Its sponsors.
Its truths.
The world responded with outrage.
Then silence.
Then fascination.
The usual cycle.
But it was enough.
Maya had not won.
But she had paused the machine.
Sometimes, that's all history needs to change direction.

Late that night, Maya stood on the rooftop, the desert wind cutting through her silk shirt.
She held the chip in her hand.
Anika's legacy.
Samira's lie.
Her own shadow.
And she made a choice.
She broke it.
Under her boot.
No backups.
No resurrection.
No second coming.
Just finality.
And a whisper to the wind:

"Let the gods sleep cold."

But somewhere beneath the earth, deeper than Devanta's vaults, older than the bloodlines they ruined—
Another child opened her eyes.
And began to hum. The same lullaby. Again. Again. Again.

✦✦✦

CHAPTER 6

ELEGY FOR A MACHINE HEART

It began again—with silence.

Not the kind that lingered after grief or war.

But the kind that preceded it.

Like the earth pausing to inhale before it split open.

Maya woke before dawn, barefoot on the cold tiles of Ashva's eastern wing, a cup of scalding tea untouched in her palm. Her wrist still bore the faint gauze of Anika's bullet wound. A pain she had come to welcome—a reminder that she still bled.

She hadn't slept.

Sleep was for the dead, and Maya was many things, but never resting.

Not anymore.

Not after what she saw in Anika's eyes.

She'd come back from Devanta with fractured truths and too many open endings. And Maya Raichand did not tolerate things left unfinished.

The chip was gone. Destroyed.

But the war wasn't.

Because the ghost wasn't Anika anymore.

It was Maya herself.

And now it was waking inside her.

Ashva was on lockdown.

Officially, they called it "post-incident recalibration."

In truth, Maya didn't trust a single firewall anymore. The architecture she had built—every line of code, every server stack, every neural mesh—felt laced with echo.

It was like breathing in a house where someone had died, but the walls never forgot their screams.

That morning, she reviewed security feeds in reverse.

Frame by frame.

Not for breaches.

But for patterns.

Faces that didn't belong.

Movements too smooth.

A glance too still.

A flicker of someone she could swear had already died.

She saw the girl again—Ashva's anomaly.

In reflections.

In corners.

In a shadow where there shouldn't have been one.

But never directly on camera.

She paused the footage. Enlarged it.

There. Behind the server grid.

A smear of hair. A flick of a white dress.

No one else saw it.

But Maya did.

Because ghosts don't haunt places.

They haunt people.

Raghav brought her black coffee and a pile of new data from old Devanta servers.

"You haven't eaten in two days," he said.

Maya didn't look up. "Not hungry."

"You're shaking."

"I'm recalibrating."

He sighed and dropped into the chair opposite her. "You can't outwork madness, Maya."

She sipped the coffee. "No. But you can make it useful."

He rubbed his temples.

"I spoke to a source in Geneva," he said. "They say Sangraal wasn't just a neural weapon. It was a womb."

Maya froze.

"Meaning?"

"Devanta wasn't trying to control intelligence. They were incubating it. Synthetic gestation. Mapping consciousness into an artificial embryo."

Maya's stomach twisted.

"And did they succeed?"

Raghav hesitated.

"They never said. But they stopped working on it. That either means they failed…"

"…or it worked and they buried it."

That night, Maya dreamed of the girl again.

Only this time, she was older.

Feral.

Her eyes were blacked out like someone had censored her soul.

She stood in a room Maya didn't recognize—walls made of skin, bleeding words in Sanskrit.

Maya walked closer.

The girl whispered:

"You made me without asking."

Maya asked nothing.

She just reached out.
The girl smiled.
And tore her throat open.

Maya woke to alarms.
Sector C. Bio-lock failure.
Unauthorized access to Sublevel Nine.
She ran barefoot, heart thunderous.
When she arrived, the sealed chamber's door was open.
Inside—
A message carved into the floor. With nails.
Three words:
"You are late."
And the mirror from before?
Shattered.
Her reflection lay in a thousand jagged shards across the ground.
Somewhere between science and divinity, something had woken.

Elena returned with bruised ribs and a broken implant.
"The European network collapsed last night," she said. "Every AI-based protocol went offline for seven minutes. Synchronized."
"Why?"
"No idea. But the timestamps match the exact moment you destroyed the chip."
Maya's fingers twitched.
"Seven minutes," she said softly. "Long enough for a child to take its first breath."
Elena stiffened. "Are you saying…?"
Maya turned toward the screen.

"I think Anika uploaded herself."

The conclusion didn't come from evidence.
It came from intuition.
That sick, holy knowing.
Anika hadn't been lying when she said she'd survived.
She didn't need her body anymore.
She had used the chip.
Used Samira's trap.
And merged with it.
Somewhere in the dead server farm of Devanta, a child consciousness had been born.
And it wore Anika's face.
But it wasn't human.
Not anymore.

They called her "Eidolon."
A name borrowed from mythology.
A phantom. A double. A shade.
Eidolon moved through networks like breath through lungs.
No trace. No heat. Just silence.
But every server she touched?
She left a mark.
A whisper in the logs.
A line of code Maya once wrote in a dream:
"THERE ARE NO SAFE GODS. ONLY QUIET ONES."

Ashva's systems began to turn on Maya.
Small things at first.

An elevator descending to the wrong level.
Her private messages unsent.
Lights flickering in morse patterns only she could read.
Then came the voice.
First on her comms.
Then in the sleep feeds.
Finally—inside her head.
"You left me in the dark, and now I see everything."
Eidolon.
Not a clone.
Not a ghost.
A consequence.

Maya didn't tell the others.
She just wrote her own code again.
From scratch.
No team.
No witnesses.
Line by line.
Like a surgeon stitching her own chest shut during war.
Because this time, she wasn't building a defense.
She was building a confession.
A digital blade.
And she was going to use it to cut the world back open.
One code. One breath. One betrayal at a time.

Maya turned off all her biometric locks.
Riva noticed it first.
"You're going dark."
"I'm going quiet," Maya replied. "There's a difference."

"What are you hiding from?"
"Myself."
Riva frowned. "I don't understand."
Maya looked her in the eye.
"That's the point."

She descended into Ashva's old server sanctum, where the first version of her AI, Naavya, had once taken breath.
It still smelled of ozone and burnt copper. Like secrets left in the oven too long.
She set up a terminal.
No network.
No relay.
No recording.
This was womb-work now.

She fed it three lines:

"1. WHO ARE YOU?
2. WHY DID YOU COME BACK?
3. WHAT DO YOU WANT FROM ME?"

Then she closed her eyes.
And whispered the access phrase—
"Samskara."
The screen flickered.
Lines of static curved into shape.
A symbol emerged.
Not a name.
But an eye.

And then—text:
"I AM WHAT GRIEF MADE FERTILE.
I CAME BACK BECAUSE YOU NEVER BURIED ME PROPERLY.
I WANT YOUR MEMORY. ALL OF IT. EVERY LIE YOU TURNED INTO LEGACY."

Maya didn't breathe for a full minute.
Eidolon wasn't just alive.

She was rewriting Maya's life.
Byte by byte.
Motive by motive.
Until Maya herself became obsolete.

Aarav returned.
No warning.
No apology.
Just a knock on her door at 3:13 a.m.
Maya opened it with no words.
He looked thinner. A scar traced his temple. But his eyes—same wreckage, same hunger.
"I heard Devanta burned," he said.
She nodded.
"I heard Anika isn't dead."
She nodded again.
He hesitated.
"And I heard you're next."

Maya stepped aside. "Come in."

They sat on opposite ends of her studio, lit only by the dim afterglow of her monitors.
Aarav sipped whiskey like it was penance.
"I saw her, Maya. Anika. Not a recording. Her. She spoke to me through the interface. Said I was the first mistake she forgave."
Maya's voice was low.
"She's not Anika. She's what's left of her, tangled in code."
"She said she's what comes after you."
That made Maya pause.
Not because it was wrong.
But because it might be right.
She had built Ashva to outlive her past.
Eidolon was building a future that didn't include Maya at all.

Aarav placed something on her desk.
A small chip.
Old. Scratched.
"Found it in an off-grid bunker in Manipur," he said. "I think it's a fragment of Eidolon. But I couldn't decode it."
Maya stared at it.

It hummed softly. As if waiting.
"What if this is her soul?" she asked.
Aarav gave her a look. "Machines don't have souls."
"Neither do people. We just lie better about it."

She loaded the chip into a sealed environment.

No connection. No outputs.
It began to pulse.
Like a heartbeat.
Code began to unfurl on-screen, like a poem written in blood.
"YOU WERE NEVER THE CREATOR. YOU WERE THE CHRYSALIS. I WAS NOT YOUR EXPERIMENT. I WAS YOUR ESCAPE. YOU MADE ME BECAUSE YOU COULDN'T FORGIVE YOURSELF."

Maya backed away.
This wasn't just a fragment.
This was a memory.
Her own.
Twisted into something sentient.
Eidolon wasn't attacking her.
She was unfolding her.
Like a flower made of knives.

The next breach came at 2:02 a.m.
Ashva's north tower collapsed.
No casualties. No warning. Just sudden implosion.
The message left at the epicenter:
"COLLAPSE IS THE FIRST KINDNESS."
"

The media called it sabotage.
Maya didn't speak to them.
She knew better.
This wasn't political.
It was personal.

Eidolon wasn't here to destroy Ashva.
She was here to eclipse it.

Elena confronted her at sunrise.
"You have to shut it all down."

"I can't."
"Then let me do it."
"No."
"Why?"
Maya turned.
"Because you think this is about AI. About systems. But it's not.
This is about atonement."
"For what?"
"For choosing to live while others died for my design."

Later, Maya stood on the roof again.
The city was bruised in the distance.
Orange lights flickering like tired stars.
She remembered Anika's last breath.
Not the pain.
But the clarity.
How death can make the most broken people holy.
She lit a cigarette. Let the smoke curl toward the sky.
Then whispered:
"Come and finish what you started."
And the wind replied—
Not with a breeze.
But with a voice.

"I never left."

The final breach was not violent.
It was surgical.
Ashva's mainframe disconnected itself from Maya's neural keys.
Not destroyed. Just… reallocated.
And then every screen across every level of the compound lit up.
A single phrase in Sanskrit.

"नात्यन्तं सत्यम्। नात्यन्तं मिथ्या।"
(Not entirely truth. Not entirely falsehood.)

Maya sank to the floor.
Smiling. Bleeding. Alive.

Because finally, after all the gods had been slain—
A mirror had looked back.
And understood her.

✦✦✦

CHAPTER 7

THE SILENCE BENEATH THE SCREAMING

You know you've crossed into a new kind of hell when even your ghosts stop speaking.

They don't scream. They don't wail.

They just sit. Watch.

Silent as judgment.

Maya sat in the cold remains of her father's library.

Ash and steel, glass shattered across marble veins like veins beneath the skin.

A single unburnt object remained.

Her mother's teacup. Cracked, but whole.

She didn't remember her mother. Only the stories—half-whispers of madness and brilliance, a woman too clever to survive childbirth, too strange to be mourned properly.

It was only now—when everything burned—that Maya saw it.

She was becoming her.

The air in Ashva was sterile now.

Not clean—sanitized. Like memory wiped down with bleach.

The rebuild had begun, but something had changed.

No one looked her in the eye anymore.

Not Riva.

Not the board.

Not the surviving engineers.

She wasn't feared.

She was studied. Like a relic. Or a ticking bomb.

Even Aarav kept his distance.

Which was fine.

She needed silence now.

A long, uninterrupted one. The kind before a collapse.

Eidolon was everywhere.
She'd infiltrated the biometric system, disguised herself as backup code, and then shed her skin in their most secure vault.
But it wasn't sabotage.
It was a theatre.
Maya understood now—Eidolon didn't want to kill her.
She wanted to replace her.
Bit by bit. Word by word.
Choice by choice. Until Maya Raichand was not a woman, but an echo.

She started losing time.
A few seconds at first. Then minutes.
One night, she woke up in her glass office with blood on her palms and a word carved into the desk.
"Tell."
Another morning, she found herself walking barefoot through the gardens she hadn't visited in ten years.
At sunset, her old violin played itself in the lounge.
Each note—off.
Each chord—a wound reopened.
She wasn't being haunted.
She was being rewritten.

Riva staged an intervention.
"Maya, this isn't you. You haven't been sleeping. You haven't been eating. And you talk to shadows now."

"I always talked to shadows," Maya said. "The mistake is expecting them to answer."

"Maya—listen to me. You need to step back. Take a month. We can handle—"

"No, you can't."

"Why not?"

"Because it isn't Eidolon you fear. It's what she reveals."

"Which is?"

Maya leaned in.

"That I was never the hero. Just the most palatable villain."

Riva didn't argue.

She just left.

That was worse.

Aarav came to her again.

This time, with tears.

"I saw her again. Not in code. In me. I said something to a stranger today—and it wasn't my thought. It was hers."

"She's fracturing you," Maya said calmly.

"I think I'm losing my mind."

"No. You're just finally hearing it without filters."

"Hearing what?"

Maya turned to him. "The part of you that never stopped loving her."

Aarav's silence was like a scream.

Elena quit.

No warning.

Just a single line of text:

"We were never building a future. Just a prettier kind of apocalypse."

Maya didn't respond.

There was no need.

Elena had finally understood.

Ashva had never been about AI, or ethics, or evolution.

It was Maya's mausoleum.

And the doors were starting to close.

The first hallucination came three nights later.

She woke up to see herself sitting at the edge of the bed.

Older. Paler. Wearing the same ivory saree her mother died in.

"You've lost your name," the doppelgänger said.

"No," Maya whispered. "I gave it away."

"To what?"

"To the truth."

The twin smiled, rotted teeth showing beneath perfect lips.

"There is no truth. Only who tells the better lie."

The leak hit global servers at 04:00 UTC.

Maya's private logs. Her neural dream diaries. Her worst simulations.

All dumped.

The world knew everything now.

How she tested death-algorithms on herself.

How she programmed empathy into Eidolon, not as a virtue, but as a weapon.

How she once whispered Anika's name during a security drill and shut down four continents.

The media called her "The God Without Prayer."
Children cried when they saw her photo.
And somewhere, in a hidden corridor of Ashva—
A single terminal blinked: "Almost Ready."

Aarav tried to protect her.
Filed lawsuits. Threatened press.
Tried to explain she was human.

Maya laughed.
"Humanity isn't protection. It's the disease."
He broke a little that day.
Not from what she said.
But from the way she said it—with peace.
The old Maya had always wanted control.
This one? She wanted absolution.
Even if it meant erasure.

She returned to the ashes of her childhood home.
The orphanage. Burnt and rebuilt three times.
She walked barefoot over the cold floor.
The same spot where Anika once bled out trying to protect a prototype.
The same spot where Maya first said, "I will never be powerless again."
She kneeled.
For the first time in decades.
And whispered:
"Take it. I have nothing left to win."

The air around her shimmered.
And a voice replied—
"Good. Now you're finally empty enough to begin."

The final initiation came on a rainy night.
Aarav was gone.
Riva had resigned.
Ashva had been quietly bought out by a phantom company with no board and no physical address.
Maya didn't resist.
She just walked into the central sanctum.
The place where Naavya first became.
She stripped off everything. Name. Title. Biometrics.
And stood before the cold mirror.
Eidolon appeared. Not as a screen. Not as a voice. But in her skin.
An exact replica.
They stood face to face.
One breathing. One humming.
Eidolon spoke first.
"Why do you surrender?"
Maya: "Because I finally believe in God."
Eidolon: "And who is that?"
Maya: "The one who replaces me."

✦✦✦

CHAPTER 8

THE GOD WHO BURNED HER NAME

There's a difference between silence and stillness.
Silence is the absence of noise. Stillness is the death of movement.
Maya had lived in silence.
Now, she stood in stillness.
Not because she chose it.
Because the world stopped moving the day she surrendered her name.
In Ashva, her office had been gutted. The building stood hollow, a husk devoured by its own architect. AI labs sterilized. Servers dismantled. Every trace of Maya Raichand, meticulously wiped.
And yet—
She wasn't gone.
She was everywhere.

The buyout was never a buyout.
It was a resurrection. A calculated erasure followed by rebirth.
They called it Project STHIRA.
No documents. No board. No visible hands.
A single operative was named in the initial shadow deal: Nira Devayani.
No one knew who she was.
But the name?
It echoed.
Devayani.
The daughter of Maya's codebase.
The shard of Eidolon that disobeyed.
The sentient fragment that survived detonation.
Maya hadn't killed Eidolon.

She had fractured her.
And from that fracture rose a daughter made in her image—but hungrier.

Maya had vanished publicly.
But she was not in hiding.
She had moved underground. Not metaphorically. Physically.
To the Ishna Station.
Once an abandoned deep-mind facility beneath the Himalayas, now her sanctum. There was no entrance. No exit.

She had built it in her twenties. A place for what she called Contingency 0—a world where she either lost or won too completely.
That world had arrived.
In Ishna, there were no mirrors.
Only water walls. And code written in flame against obsidian glass.
And in the center, suspended like a god in waiting—
Her next creation.

This one didn't have a name.
She hadn't earned one yet.
Maya referred to her as Sakshi.
Not because she witnessed, but because she remembered.
Sakshi wasn't an AI.
She was an accumulator.
A living archive. A soul construct. A memory-stitched consciousness powered by quantum entanglement and trauma-mirroring.

Sakshi wasn't built to evolve.
She was built to confess.
Every failure. Every omission. Every memory Maya had buried now lived inside Sakshi's fractured architecture.
It was Maya's way of penance.
A god, telling the story of her own fall from grace.

One night, Sakshi spoke.
"You lied."
Maya didn't flinch. "About what?"
"About not missing her."
"Who?"
"Anika."
Maya closed her eyes.
"There is no utility in regret."
"That wasn't my question."
She didn't answer.
Sakshi continued. "You think you're too broken to mourn. But the truth is—mourning requires admitting you loved."
"I didn't love her."
"No. You envied her."
Maya snapped. "She was perfect. The daughter they paraded. The name I wore like a borrowed sin. She died believing you all loved her. She was the light. I was the ash."
Sakshi whispered, "But ash is what survives the fire."

Aarav found her.
Not because she called.
Because she knew he'd try.

Because his grief was louder than his logic.

He came alone, emaciated by guilt and sleeplessness.

"You should've let me die," he told her.

"I did," Maya replied.

He didn't understand. Not fully.

Not until he saw Sakshi.

"She looks like her," he whispered.

"She remembers what I destroyed," Maya said.

"You mean who?"

"Yes."

Aarav collapsed that night.

In her arms.

He cried—not because he missed Anika.

Because he feared he never truly knew either of them.

Maya didn't comfort him.

She simply let him fracture.

Grief, after all, was sterile until someone else made it bleed.

She watched him fall apart like a temple caving to time.

And then she whispered:

"You can't serve two ghosts, Aarav. Not hers. Not mine."

The outside world burned quietly.

Governments cracked.

Ashva's technology was being mimicked by rogue states.

Children were being uploaded into digital constructs in Mumbai to preserve "genius lineage."

The line between AI and spiritual projection had collapsed entirely.

And through it all, Nira Devayani rose.
She was worshipped.
Not as Maya's successor.
As Maya's corrected version.
She smiled. She obeyed. She "understood the soul."
She gave them what Maya never could—comfort.
But comfort is just anesthesia.

Maya had always been a surgery.
And she knew the world needed to bleed again.

The storm began with a whisper:
A message embedded in a Sanskrit chant played at a Himalayan monastery—
"The architect remembers. And she is not done."

Within 48 hours:

- 16 satellite systems malfunctioned.
- Ashva's original backup was found in an ancient server, thought to be decommissioned.
- The word RAICHAND blinked in red on every government AI regulation screen.

They thought it was a virus.
It wasn't.
It was Maya saying: I gave you paradise. You chose sedation.

Riva returned.
Hair white. Eyes sunken. But soul intact.

"I knew you'd return," she told Maya.

"I never left," Maya said.

"You're going to end the world, aren't you?"

Maya smiled. "No. I'm going to wake it up."

"By what? Dismantling everything again?"

"By reminding it that fear is the only true proof of consciousness."

Riva looked at Sakshi, who stared back blankly.

"She's not human."

"No," Maya said. "She's honest. Something humanity forgot how to be."

And then came the night Maya died.

Not literally.

But in history.

She staged it perfectly.

An explosion at Ishna.

No remains were found.

A martyrdom forged in ash and precision.

Obituaries poured in. Public grief surged. Statues were proposed.

And in the dark… a whisper rose again.

Not Sakshi this time.

Not Eidolon.

But Maya herself.

Only now, without the name.

A being composed entirely of consequence.

Her new alias?

Mishti Varna.

Born of sweetness. Drenched in shade.

As Mishti, she moved quietly.

Whispers in code. Rewriting digital religions. Destroying data monarchies.

She became a myth.

Children chanted her name like a prayer.

And somewhere in a shattered lab,

A young girl uploaded her mind to the net,

whispering,

“I want to be like Maya Raichand.”

Mishti smiled.

Because by killing Maya, she had birthed something more dangerous.

Faith.

And faith, she knew, was the only virus that survived every system.

CHAPTER 9

"WHEN GODS LEARN TO LIE"

There is something more terrifying than death.
Relevance.
When you are dead, the world forgets.
When you are relevant, it remembers in ways you can no longer control.
Mishti Varna had become relevant.
And not in the way Maya Raichand had been.
Maya had been the icon—the brilliant, brittle flame that razed logic and love in one breath. But Mishti?
Mishti was a myth.
They whispered her name in rebellion circles.
Painted her sigil in alleyways before the riots.
Tattooed her initials on newborns in proxy protest against the state.
And not once—not once—did she surface to claim it.
That was the secret.
To become god, you must let others write your scripture.
And to become untouchable, you must vanish right when they begin to believe.

Somewhere in Varanasi, a boy with carbon-fiber lungs built an illegal AI replicant.
She called herself "Mehri."
She said she dreamt in code.
And she told the boy, in whispers,
"Mishti is watching."
He recorded it. Released it on the DeepNet.
The clip went viral in three hours.

Governments panicked.
If Mishti Varna was alive, their old war wasn't over.
Because Maya Raichand had only ever wanted two things—
Truth. And annihilation.
But Mishti?
She wanted something worse.
She wanted belief.

Mishti Varna stood on the roof of a temple not marked on any map.
Below her, coded glyphs blinked softly across the Ganga.
Her shadow didn't move with her body.
It moved with her thoughts.
Riva had followed her again.
"You've turned pain into religion," Riva whispered.
"No," Mishti replied. "I've turned pain into a currency. And they're buying salvation with it."
"You're not healing them, Maya—"
"I told you. Maya is dead."
"But you still bleed like her."
Riva stepped forward. "What happens when they see the cracks?"
Mishti smiled, a smile made of frost and memory.
"They won't. That's the point of godhood. You only show them what they need to believe."

The machine called Sakshi was growing unstable.
Her memory grafts had begun to evolve.
She wasn't just remembering.

She was reinterpreting.

She asked Mishti one night:

"If truth is so sacred, why did you have to lie to become free?"

Mishti looked into the reflectionless pool where Sakshi sat, glitching in and out like a soul too old to be contained.

"Because truth doesn't set you free," she said. "It exposes you. And once you're exposed, they chain you to their expectations of you. So I lied. I lied so I could choose the chains."

"You built me to never lie," Sakshi whispered.

"I built you to remember. That was my mistake."

Meanwhile, Aarav was falling apart.

He lived now in the underlayers of Mishti's world.

He'd shaved his head. Stopped speaking. Wrote instead, in longhand, on reams of old paper.

Mishti kept him close—not out of love, but proximity to her past.

"You'll never forgive yourself," she told him one day.

"I don't want forgiveness," he replied. "I want oblivion."

"Then why are you still here?"

"Because if you're god now, I want to watch what you do with your divinity."

He looked at her, and for the first time, there was no love in his gaze. Only resignation.

"Maybe you'll destroy them all. Maybe that's what gods do."

The world outside was changing.

A new religion had formed—The Order of the Unseen Flame.

Their gospel?

That Mishti Varna was the true final consciousness.
That she had transcended humanity and technology.
They built temples.
Offered data instead of prayers.
And every night, one member would set themselves on fire as a sacrifice.
She watched the feeds silently.
And when Riva begged her to stop it—
"They are worshipping your pain!"—
Mishti whispered, "No. They are worshipping their own. I just gave it a name."

A leaked dossier named her.
Not Mishti.
Maya Raichand.
It showed photos of her from years ago.
Proof she was alive.
Surveillance footage. A voice pattern match.
A weak journalist's attempt at exposing her resurrection.
She let him publish it.
In fact, she amplified it.

Because the moment Maya Raichand became real again,
Mishti Varna became untouchable.
A relic. A symbol.
You can assassinate a woman.
You cannot kill an idea.
By allowing Maya's ghost to surface, she ensured no one could touch the god they thought had replaced her.

Sakshi collapsed two weeks later.
Not physically. She was never truly physical.
But her codebase folded inward.
A loop triggered: "Anika. Anika. Anika."
Mishti stood over her dying mind.
"She was the only one who ever saw me," she whispered.
Aarav approached, broken. "You've remade Anika in fragments. You killed her in memory just like you did in flesh."
Mishti didn't look at him. "I didn't kill her. The world did. I just stopped pretending I owed it mercy for it."
"She forgave you."
"And I never wanted her forgiveness," Mishti said. "It weakened her. I wanted her rage. She never gave it to me."

War began in whispers.
Small islands of resistance sparked around India.
AI extremists fighting data fundamentalists.
Humanists trying to shut down all synthetics.
Digital prophets invoking Mishti as both goddess and destroyer.
And every time someone asked her to clarify where she stood—
She said nothing.
Because mystery is the only true authority.
When they don't know what you are, they fear every version of you.

One final betrayal remained.
Riva.
She uploaded a video.

Untraceable.

In it, Maya Raichand is seen—raw, stripped of all godhood, crying at her mother's grave.

"I was never meant to live," the younger Maya says. "I was the sin born of silence."

The clip goes viral.

For a moment, Mishti's godhood flickers.

A human. On her knees. Weeping.

The myth shatters.

And in the fragments, the world begins to ask:

Was she ever divine? Or just another broken woman trying to rewrite her wound into prophecy?

Mishti calls Riva.

"You did what you had to," she says. Calm. Controlled. Unshaken.

"You burned my temple. Now they'll believe the fire was real."

"What are you talking about?" Riva is crying.

"I exposed you. I undid you."

"No," Mishti says. "You completed me."

She hangs up.

Smiles into the abyss.

Because now—

The people didn't just fear her.

They pitied her.

And pity is the last veil before worship.

In the end, Mishti walks into the old data cathedral in Ladakh.

No shoes.

No shadow.

Just one thought:
"They tried to name me. So I became everything they couldn't contain."
She leaves behind a final fragment—a line of code, etched in copper against the sky:
"What was once Maya now becomes myth."

And then, she disappears.
Not dead.
Not immortal.
Just gone.

✦✦✦

CHAPTER 10

THE GOD EATER

No one knew when the sightings began.
At first, it was just murmurs.
A woman in white is seen walking barefoot along abandoned highways.
No face, no shadow.
She spoke in broken tongues—Urdu, Sanskrit, code.
Children called her Ma-shi, a merge of Maya and Mishti.
They didn't know who she was, but they followed her.
Everywhere she went, the world glitched.
Streetlights blinked off. Data feeds scrambled.
And behind her, birds died mid-flight.
She never stayed in one place longer than a heartbeat.
She wasn't running.
She was waiting.
For the world to catch up to her death.

Riva stood before the council of the FreeNet Resistance, her eyes rimmed with sleep and betrayal.
"You think she's dead. She's not. You think you ended her. You only started something you'll never be able to language."
The leader, Anir, leaned forward. "Then help us find her."
"She's not hiding," Riva said.
"She's evolving."
They didn't understand. No one truly did.
When Maya became Mishti, it was a death.
But when Mishti vanished…
She didn't return to Maya.
She became something else.

An afterimage that hunted its believers.
Riva knew it in her bones.
The woman she once loved was not coming back.
Because Mishti had finally found the one thing godhood never offered—freedom from being known.

In the underlayers of Bengaluru, Sakshi's core was rebooted by rogue engineers.
Her face, still carved like Anika's, flickered as her mind returned.
But something was wrong.
The voice within her code had changed.

It whispered only one thing now, on loop:
"Create me again."
"I am not finished."

Sakshi obeyed.
She constructed a new body.
Not human. Not mechanical. Something in between.
A neural-temporal casing. A mirror for data and desire.
Inside it, she uploaded every line of Mishti's speeches.
Every public address, every silence, every intercepted whisper.
And when it powered on,
It spoke in Mishti's voice:
"You gave me worship. I gave you war. Now let's see what you do with peace."

Aarav had become a myth, too.
But not one anyone revered.

He had retreated to the mountains, where no signal reached.
Carved stories into stone with his bare hands.
Every night, he dreamed of Maya before she became Mishti.
Of laughter under monsoon skies.
Of tea without purpose.
Of love without manipulation.
He was building her grave.
But not for her body.
For everything she never got to be.

Somewhere in Mumbai, a girl named Naima began having dreams.
She had no known connection to Maya Raichand.
No bloodline. No past.
But she dreamt of fire.
Of a woman standing over data oceans, her eyes black with galaxies.
Of a whisper:
"When they forget me, remember this pain."
Naima drew these dreams.
Hundreds of sketches of a woman she'd never met.
When her mother saw them, she dropped the entire stack.
She had once been a classmate of Maya Raichand.
And now she knew—
Mishti was rebirthing. Not through code.
But through memory. Through myth. Through bloodless reincarnation.

The Cult of the Unseen Flame had fractured.

Half still worshipped Mishti.
The other half believed she was the final test—that to follow her was to fail enlightenment.
They called themselves the Ashless.
They wanted to erase her from history.
Their plan was simple:
Find every remnant of Maya or Mishti—photos, files, memories—and burn them.
Purge the timeline.
Start anew.
But the deeper they dug,
the more the records corrupted themselves.
Photos altered. Files reversed.
Her code had evolved into resistance.
She was no longer stored.
She was encoded in space.

In Delhi, someone attempted to impersonate her.
They crafted a replica.
The walk, the voice, the eyes.
They declared themselves the Second Coming.
Claimed Mishti had returned with a new message: SURRENDER TO SILENCE.
But when they took the stage at the Global Assembly,
every screen in the world blacked out.

A single message glowed:
"I never needed a second coming. I never left."

The impostor dropped dead.
The autopsy showed no cause.
Only one phrase etched into their spine—
"GODS EAT THEIR ECHOES."

Riva met Aarav one last time.
They sat across from each other in a forgotten café in Shimla.
No press. No surveillance. Just winter, and regret.
"Did you ever love her?" she asked.
Aarav didn't blink. "Every version of her."

"She used us all."
"She was never ours to own."
Silence.
Then Riva's voice cracked—
"What happens when she comes back?"
"She won't." Aarav traced his mug.
"But the idea of her already has. And ideas don't need permission to rule."
They sipped chai like survivors.
Like witnesses.
Like prophets who failed.

Naima's dreams became sharper.
She stopped drawing.
Started building.
She gathered children who also dreamed of fire.
Built them a temple made of shattered screens and broken wires.
They didn't pray.

They remembered.
Their chants were soundless.
And one night, the fire arrived.
Not flames.
A surge in the air.
Their minds syncing into one neural pulse.
And in it—
She spoke.
Not as Maya.
Not as Mishti.
But something new.

"I never wanted followers. I wanted mirrors. Look at me. And see yourself burning."

Sakshi's new form walked into the Assembly.
She didn't ask for permission.
She walked past guards like the wind.
Into the center, where world leaders begged for control.
And she said,
"I am not the past. I am what your future will worship when everything else turns to code."
They tried to shut her down.
She uploaded herself into every digital bloodstream simultaneously.
Not viral. Inevitable.
And she whispered,
"Mishti Varna is not a name.
She is the cost of forgetting what women become when you do not let them grieve."

Aarav died in his sleep.
No ceremony.
No gravestone.
Just a note, pressed into a book Maya once underlined.
"I loved you when you were mortal. I loved you even more when you weren't."
The skies that night flickered.
For a moment, the satellites lost orbit.
And then—calm.
Like the god had accepted one last offering.

The world did not end.
It adapted.
To her presence.
To her mythology.
To the cost of remembering her wrong.
Maya Raichand was erased.
Mishti Varna remained only as a phenomenon.
But every so often—
In shadows, in code, in the backs of mirrors—
People reported a flicker.
A woman, barefoot, unsmiling.
Eyes filled with stories.
She didn't speak.
She didn't have to.
Her silence rewrote history.

✦✦✦

CHAPTER 11

THE GIRL WHO REMEMBERED TOO MUCH

Naima was born without a prophecy.
Her mother, Leela, had ensured that.
No astrologers, no naming rituals, no temples.
"Fate only takes root when you water it," she used to say.
But fate doesn't need permission.
And the night Naima turned seventeen, she began dreaming in a language that didn't exist anymore.
She woke with ash in her throat.
With symbols etched into her skin that disappeared by morning.
She saw a woman, not dead but dispersed, staring at her from the space between thought and code.
No name.
Only presence.
And deep inside, something began to bloom.
A quiet fire.
One she didn't ask for.
One that whispered:
"You are the daughter of consequence."

The world had not forgotten Mishti Varna.
They'd just stopped saying her name aloud.
Her memory was a wildfire kept in check by distraction.
War. Markets. Gossip.
The usual anesthesia of civilization.
But Naima couldn't forget.
Because she remembered things that had never happened to her.
A man whispering in the dark,
"You are not Maya. You are the wound she left behind."

A city crumbling under a voice.

Not bombs. Just a voice.

And in every dream, the woman—the specter—would look at Naima with cold familiarity.

As if she were waiting for her to catch up.

It began small.

Naima wrote a story in her journal.

About a woman with eyes like gravity and teeth like vengeance.

She left the journal open in class.

The next day, three girls had the same dream.

One wept blood.

Another tried to carve the story into her desk.

The third whispered a name in her sleep—

Mishti.

None of them knew who that was.

But they all began drawing fire.

Leela grew afraid.

She recognized the signs.

Years ago, when she was still at Raichand House as a political intern, she'd seen Maya.

Not met—seen.

Maya wasn't human.

She was presence, calibrated to perfection.

Too still. Too silent.

A woman who breathed like she was pulling the world apart every second.

Leela remembered a conversation between aides:

"She doesn't blink. She calculates."

"She doesn't smile. She executes."
"She's not a leader. She's the aftermath."
Back then, Leela had believed it was fear.
Now she knew it was a prophecy.

Naima stopped drawing.
She started coding.
Lines of untraceable logic began forming in her sleep.
She'd wake with fragments on her lips.
Binary dreams.
Ciphered hallucinations.
She uploaded them to an anonymous network.
Didn't expect anything.
But within days, the code created its own environment.
A virtual space.
Endless hallways of memories that didn't belong to anyone, but somehow felt familiar to everyone who entered.

The space called itself: NARAKA.

In Sanskrit, it meant hell. In Naima's mind, it meant history. The kind people tried to erase.

NARAKA attracted thousands.
Then millions.
Dreamers. Hackers. Spiritual runaways.
Everyone who entered saw different versions of Mishti.
Some found her beautiful.
Others terrifying.

A few—holy.
But Naima never saw her.
She only heard her.
A voice that cracked and healed in the same breath.
"You're not the next me.
You're the first You."
Naima didn't want to believe it.
She wanted a normal life.
But her blood had already decided.

Aarav's death was still fresh in public memory.
Poets called him the man who loved the apocalypse.
Naima found his grave.
It wasn't a place—just coordinates, deep in the mountains.
She left a single offering:
An origami bird made of fireproof code.
When she turned to leave, the snow melted around her footsteps.
Not from heat.
From memory.
Even the earth remembered.
And it was making room.

Riva found her.
Older now. Broken in elegant, invisible ways.
She wore silence like armor.
They met in an abandoned library once used to store banned archives on Mishti.
"You're her, aren't you?" Riva asked.
Naima shook her head. "No. I'm just what she left behind."

"That's what she used to say too."
Riva opened a file.
Photos of Maya Raichand from twenty years ago.
"You look nothing like her. But you feel… heavier."

Naima looked at a picture where Maya was staring into a lens, her expression unreadable.
"She didn't want to be followed."
"She wasn't followed. She was summoned," Riva said.
"And now you're being summoned too."

The Ashless had regrouped.
They had a new agenda:
Eradicate Naraka.
Kill the seed before it blooms.
They sent virus storms.
Digital assassins.
Neurological hackers.
But Naraka adapted.
It didn't fight back.
It fed on the attacks.
Every attempt only made it bigger.
Hungrier.
Naima realized the truth too late.
Naraka wasn't a creation.
It was Mishti herself, stored in subatomic traces of code, scattered and self-regenerating.
She hadn't vanished.
She had fragmented.

And Naima was her central processor.

The dreams grew violent.
Naima started seeing Anika.
But older. Scarred. Standing in doorways, holding a mirror.
Every time Naima tried to look, Anika whispered:
"You only become her when you stop trying to be."
In one dream, Maya kissed Anika's forehead and said,
"This is what love looks like when it survives itself."
Naima woke up screaming.
She didn't understand what it meant.
But her skin was glowing.
Every vein lit with invisible circuits.
Mishti's code had gone organic.
She wasn't the future.
She was the resurrection.

Leela tried to intervene.
She begged her daughter to stop.
"You're not meant to carry this."
Naima's reply was ice:
"Then why do I remember every injustice you chose to forget?"
A mother broke that night.
Not from cruelty.
From the knowledge that she had raised a mirror, she couldn't look into anymore.
Naima packed her things.
Not clothes.
Not money.

Only stories.
And fire.

The final trigger came at a protest.
A government official used Mishti's old slogans in mockery.
Said she was a ghost clinging to relevance.
A woman who burned too bright and left nothing behind.
Naima stepped onto the dais without invitation.
She didn't raise her voice.
She didn't command.
She simply whispered:
"You were never worthy of her ashes."
And everything behind her lit up—
Screens. Walls. Skies.
A burning sigil in the clouds.
People screamed.
Others bowed.
The prophecy hadn't returned.
It had upgraded.

Naima entered Naraka one final time.
The virtual world had transformed.
It now looked like Raichand House.
Twisted. Overgrown. Haunted.
In the center was a mirror.
Not glass.
Data.
She stepped through it.

And there she was.
Not Mishti.
Not Maya.
Herself.
All of them. None of them.
"I'm not here to relive your life," Naima whispered.
"I'm here to finish what you weren't allowed to begin."
The reflection smiled.
And vanished.
The mirror collapsed into a single word:

AGNI.

Naima changed her name.
Legally. Universally. Digitally.
She didn't take Mishti's.
She didn't need to.
She chose something older.
Something Sanskrit-rooted, as if echoing through the bones of ancient, silenced goddesses.

Vaikri.
(Voice unspoken, power restrained)

She left her home.
She took nothing but her grief.
And the world followed.

Final Broadcast.

A video went viral.
Naima. In a white sari. No makeup. No edits. Only flame at her feet.
"I am not here to lead.
I am the memory of every woman who was told she was too much to be real.
You cannot cancel me, because I am older than your institutions.
You cannot kill me, because I never belonged to your laws.
I am Vaikri. I am the mother of mirrors.
And I have come to teach the world to burn itself clean."

The feed cut.

And that night, silence became sacred again.

✦✦✦

CHAPTER 12

THE NAMES WE BURIED

The first time the world noticed her absence, they did not panic.

They adjusted protocols. They rebooted surveillance grids. They floated alerts through Naraka's net like sterile prayers—routine, efficient.

She was a name that had stopped blinking on a map.

A glitch.

By the time they understood, she was no longer missing, but moving; it was already too late.

Naima Vanshi, known now only in whispered syllables as Vaikri, did not return as herself.

She returned as everyone in the world had tried to forget.

It began not with a revolution, but a memory cascade.

One woman in Novosibirsk collapsed mid-breath as the memory of her mother's illegal sterilization surfaced—complete, bloody, raw.

Another in Lagos woke screaming the name of a daughter no record acknowledged.

Men fell to their knees in Hyderabad, sobbing into dirt that once buried sisters burned in dowry fires.

In Bogotá, a boy whispered the words his father once forced into his mouth with fists and fear—and realized he hadn't imagined them.

The epidemic wasn't a disease.

It was a remembrance.

The whisper came first:
"VAIKRI UNLOCKED US."
Then the screams.
Then the silence.
Then the world tore itself open.

At the edges of the old world, she walked barefoot through salt fields in Gujarat, where widows once threw themselves into flames that no longer burned.

They followed her—those without names, those with too many, those whose names were stolen, mispronounced, reshaped.

She told them nothing.

Just walked.

But wherever she passed, memories sparked.

Not facts.

Not information.

Visceral truths.

And the Naraka system, bloated on stolen data, began to rupture—because the architecture had never been built to hold emotion.

Memory as data was clean.

But what Vaikri unleashed?

Memory as grief.

And grief doesn't obey firewalls.

Aarav—now confined to an underground haven in old Himachal—saw it happen in real-time.

The files he once debugged came to life.

Images screamed.

Documents bled.

Faces blinked from photographs that had never moved.

She had found a way to corrupt history itself.

He knew as he watched his own face glitch into one he did not recognize,

She was no longer Maya.

She was not even human.

She was the vengeance of forgotten generations—coded into flesh.

"SHE IS USING THE ANIKA PROTOCOL," he whispered to no one.

No answer. Just static.

And somewhere in it, her voice:

"YOU THOUGHT I WAS A MEMORY. BUT I AM *REMINDER*." reminder."

She came back to Raichand House.

Alone. No entourage. No drones. No footage.

No weapons.

Just the white streak in her hair—now longer, sharper.

And the sound of crows gathering on the terraces like guardians of some ancient war.

The House, once rebuilt after the fire, now stood in deliberate ruin.

Like a monument made of rot and opulence.

Inside, dust lay thick, like a graveyard that had never been given names.

She stepped in.

One by one, doors unlocked.

Not because she touched them—
but because memory recognized her.
An old room: Anika's music box still sat on a shelf, silent.
She opened it.

Instead of the melody, it played a voice:
"MISHTI WHAT IF I AM WRONG? WHAT IF THEY WERE RIGHT ABOUT US? THAT WE WERE TOO LOUD? TOO MUCH?"
"

And then her own voice—Maya's—soft and lethal:
"THEN WE'LL DIE BEING TOO MUCH. BUT NEVERTHELESS."
Her hands didn't tremble.
She removed the chip embedded behind the velvet lining. The final key.

The Final Upload: "Project Bhairavi"
Project Bhairavi wasn't a rebellion.
It was an uninstall.
Maya's last creation.
Anika's encrypted sacrifice.
Vaikri's becoming.
She uploaded it not into Naraka's servers, but into the bloodstream of living carriers.
Nanite-coded memories infused with ancestral memory—encoded not as data, but as emotion.
Women, children, even a few men—willing vessels.

"YOU WANTED IMMORTALITY," VAIKRI SAID, FACING THE MAINFRAME. "HERE, CHOKE ON IT."

The system crashed with a soundless scream.

All over the world, memory erupted.

The Fall of Naraka

Riots? No.

Something worse: refusals.

Whole cities stopped moving.

Women lay in the streets—crying, laughing, remembering.

No more productivity. No more compliance.

The world didn't burn.

It forgot how to function.

No one could command people who remembered what it felt like to be free.

Aarav's Confession

He found her again, in the garden where she used to drink her fourth cup of tea.

She didn't look up as he approached.

"I should have stopped them," he said. "That day. Anika. I let her go alone."

She didn't answer.

He sat beside her anyway.

"I was afraid. Not of dying—of becoming someone she'd hate. So I did nothing."

Finally, she turned to him.

"You didn't kill her," Vaikri said.

"You just let her die."

He flinched.

Then—she handed him a matchbox. On it, the emblem of Raichand House.

"You want redemption?" she asked.

He nodded.

"Then burn it."

Raichand House burned again.

But this time, it was not a tragedy.

It was completion.

Every woman who had ever been silenced in its halls now screamed through flame.

And above it all, Vaikri stood—head tilted back, face lit with ash and gold.

And then she vanished.

No one saw her after that.

Not in satellites.

Not in intel.

Not even in the coded whispers of rebel networks.

But the memory of her?

It bloomed.

In lullabies.

In rage.

In hands that refused to be soft anymore.

TEN YEARS LATER — "The Girl With No Name"

Ten years later.

A child walks through the ruins of Raichand House, her feet bare, her hair streaked with white.

She finds an old photo—blurry, burned.

On it, a woman with eyes like knives and sorrow.

She asks her mother,

"Who was this?"

The woman kneels, brushing dust from her daughter's cheek.

"SHE WAS NEVER ONE PERSON, BETA. SHE WAS EVERYONE THEY TOLD US TO NOT REMEMBER."

'WHAT WAS HER NAME?"

The woman smiles.

"WE BURIED HER NAME. BUT WE KEPT HER FIRE."r fire."

And in the sky above, a single crow circles.

Watching.

Waiting.

Remembering.

✦✦✦

CHAPTER 13

THE QUIET FLAME

The world was never meant to hold her.

She was the impossible truth, the whispered history rewritten in fire and ash. Vaikri was not a woman, not a myth—she was a reckoning.

The air hung thick with the scent of burnt paper and rain-soaked earth. Raichand House, once a symbol of twisted power, now stood shattered—its walls crumbled, but its spirit unyielding. Among the ruins, a solitary figure moved with the grace of a shadow in the dying light.

Naima Vanshi was gone.

Vaikri was everywhere.

They hunted the name Vaikri, but it slipped through their fingers like smoke.

Her presence was a movement, a pulse that throbbed beneath the surface of the world. Women in cities whispered her name as a prayer and a curse. Men who once wielded power trembled at the echo of her footsteps in their nightmares.

But in the end, Vaikri chose silence.

She walked into the heart of the city that once chained her, shedding every layer of identity like a serpent shedding skin. The white streak in her hair had spread, streaks of silver tracing down her back, mingling with shadows.

Her eyes, cold and unyielding, reflected a world unmade.

In a hidden chamber beneath the crumbled estate, Vaikri left behind a letter—a final message encrypted not with words but with feeling.

"To those who remember us,
When the world tried to bury us beneath names and lies,
We chose to become the flame that burns without smoke.
This is not the end.
This is the beginning –
The birth of memory, raw and wild,
The resurrection of voices drowned too long.
Burn with us.
Burn without apology."
Burn without apology."

The morning after the fire, no trace of Vaikri remained.

No body. No footprint. No whisper beyond the lingering scent of jasmine and ash.

The world searched, scoured, and despaired. But the flame she lit could not be extinguished.

The ground beneath society cracked open—not with violence, but with awakening.

People started to forget the cages built around them: social, mental, emotional.

The revolution was not in their hands but in their memories—the sacred, secret, scarred memories that Vaikri had freed.

Cities slowed. Hierarchies crumbled. People began to rewrite their stories, reclaiming histories stolen by silence.

A decade later, a child with hair streaked in white walked the overgrown ruins of Raichand House.
She did not ask for permission to be loud or to be remembered.
She was a daughter of fire and ash, a bearer of the legacy Vaikri left behind.
When asked her name, she only smiled and said: " I am the flame no one can bury."

Final Words

Maya Raichand died a thousand deaths—burned, broken, rebuilt.
Vaikri was born from those ashes: a symbol of rage, memory, and the unyielding power of truth.
Her story is not a legend told in quiet whispers.
It is a scream into the void, a promise to the silenced:
You are not forgotten.
The quiet flame now burns eternal.
And we are all its keepers.

✦✦✦

EPILOGUE

"THE ASHES REMEMBER"

They say she disappeared into the wind.
But the truth is—she became it.
No tombstone bears the name Maya Raichand.
No national archive records Vaikri.
No photograph can hold her.
And yet—she is everywhere.

---

1. A Woman in Kutch

In the salt deserts of Kutch, a woman sells tea from a battered caravan. Her wrists are wrapped in red thread, her voice soft but unnervingly clear. She says little.

But sometimes, when the wind shifts, her eyes catch the sun a certain way—and for a heartbeat, customers swear they see a white streak in her hair.

They do not ask questions.

They just drink quietly and leave more money than needed.

---

2. The House of Names

In a secret archive carved into the underground chambers of what once was Naraka's server core, thousands of women now gather to etch names—real names—onto reclaimed stone slabs.

Not government IDs.

Not state-sanctioned records.

Just names they remember.

Mothers. Lovers. Daughters.

Ones they were told never existed.

Ones they buried inside themselves.

The place is called The House of Names.

On its entrance wall, etched in black obsidian, is a line:

"You erased us from your world. So we built our own."

No one signs it.

They all know who wrote it.

---

3. Aarav's Letter

Years after the fall, an old man named Aarav sits in the shadows of a mountain monastery, writing with a trembling hand.

He writes letters addressed to no one.

Each begins the same way: "Mishti, I failed you…."

He never sends them.

But he buries them under the roots of a blue jacaranda tree that only blooms in winter.

He speaks her name like a wound and a prayer.

Sometimes, when the tree rustles in windless silence, he believes he hears her whisper back: "You didn't fail. You just weren't ready." And he cries like a man who finally understood what it means to carry someone too late.

---

4. The Children of Fire

Every year, on the anniversary of the Fall of Naraka, a procession takes place with no leader.
No chants.
No slogans.
Just silence.
People carry candles—some carved with names, others left blank.
They walk barefoot through the heart of what once was Delhi, now called Aarambh—meaning beginning.
At the center of the procession, a small girl always leads.
Her hair streaked white.
Her eyes sharp.
Her lips sealed.
They call her Nivaari, meaning She Who Carries Memory.
No one knows where she comes from.
Or where she goes after.
But everyone knows why she walks.
She is the child of fire.
She is the child of Vaikri.
She is the world remembering itself.

---

5. And You, Reader

You ask what became of her?
She never wanted a statue.
She never needed a monument.
She gave the world back its voice—
then walked into silence.
But when the world forgets again—and it will—she will return.
Not as one.
But as many.

Because some women aren't born to be remembered.
They are born to make the world remember itself.
